GNOME
ALONE
at Christmas

With special thanks to Jonny Leighton

ORCHARD BOOKS

First published in Great Britain in 2023 by Hodder & Stoughton

1 3 5 7 9 10 8 6 4 2

Text © Hodder & Stoughton Limited 2023
Cover and inside illustrations by Di Brookes
© Hodder & Stoughton Limited 2023

A CIP catalogue record for this book is available from the British Library.

ISBN 978 1 40837 154 1

Printed in Great Britain

MIX
Paper from
responsible sources
FSC® C104740

The paper and board used in this book are made from
wood from responsible sources

Orchard Books
An imprint of Hachette Children's Group
Part of Hodder & Stoughton Limited
Carmelite House, 50 Victoria Embankment, London EC4Y 0DZ

An Hachette UK Company
www.hachette.co.uk
www.hachettechildrens.co.uk

GNOME ALONE

at Christmas

NICK PINE

Illustrated by Di Brookes

Contents

Chapter One

There wasn't a boy in the world who loved Christmas as much as Noah Gibson. In fact, there wasn't a girl in the world who loved Christmas as much as Noah Gibson. Actually, there wasn't a man, woman, cat, dog, hamster, hippo, horse, mouse, dinosaur, donkey, dung beetle or duck that loved Christmas as much as Noah

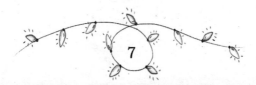

Gibson. (And that's saying something, because ducks go quackers for pulling Christmas crackers.)

Noah loved Christmas so much that he had a special Advent calendar with so many doors on it he had to begin opening them in August. He loved

Christmas so much that he listened to Christmas carols on repeat with the family cat, Mrs Jingles, until she was miaowing the words along with him. He loved it so much that on his birthday, he ate Christmas pudding instead of double chocolate chip birthday cake.

But this year, although the nights had grown dark and cold, and the high street sparkled with twinkling lights, and the tempting smells of delicious hot drinks wafted up his nostrils wherever he went, Noah wasn't feeling very Christmassy at all.

The whole family was worried about

his grandma, who was in hospital with a poorly stomach. Noah felt a horrible feeling in his own tummy every time he thought about her. Mum and Dad had been visiting her every day, but they didn't know when she'd be able to come home.

"Don't worry, Noah. Gran's a tough old bird," Dad kept saying. "She keeps asking us to bring her some pickled herring, so she can't be feeling *that* poorly."

"Even though the smell of it is making everyone else feel sick!" Mum had added.

Pickled herring was a delicacy in Norway, the country Gran was from. She couldn't help but wolf them down when she got her hands on then, but they created some seriously powerful wind.

Something was up with Noah's older sister, Gemma, too. She used to be just as excited about Christmas as him. Well, not *quite*, but enough to bake cookies with him, wrap presents together and hang up sparkly decorations all over the house. This year, though, she hadn't done anything festive with Noah. All she did was tap

away on her phone or stomp round the house like a moody rhinoceros. (Unlike ducks, rhinos do **NOT** like Christmas.)

Noah's family had been so distracted that they'd gone through December and right up to Christmas Eve and the house was hardly even decorated. Dad had brought the tree in, but despite Noah's pleading, it didn't have a single bauble on it – instead, it looked like any old tree that you could see in any old field, except it was in the corner of the living room, slowly dropping its needles over the few presents that were scattered underneath.

As Noah, Gemma and their mum all gathered in the living room, Noah took one look at the sad old tree and sighed. So much for Christmas...

"**OWWW-AH!**" Gemma suddenly screeched, making Mrs Jingles jump up from her resting place beside the fire and scamper across the living room. "Mummm... I just got a pine needle stuck in my big toe!"

Mum was busy rummaging around in her bag and didn't seem to notice what Gemma had said at all.

"Oh, how lovely," she said. "Did you get her a gift too?"

"What?" Gemma said. "I'm talking about having a pine needle stuck in my toe, Mum, not what Christmas presents I've been getting!"

"Oh dear," said Mum. "How upsetting."

Noah giggled. If his sister had looked up from her phone for two seconds, she might have spotted that the carpet was littered with pine needles.

"Mum," he said as Gemma plonked herself down on the sofa to inspect her toe. "I brought the decoration box down from the attic. I had to fight off a couple of hundred spiders get

it. It was no big deal, obviously – it IS Christmas, after all. The thing is, I was just wondering if we could start—"

Mum finally found what she was looking for at the bottom of her bag: a set of jangly car keys.

"Noah, love," she said. "I'm sorry, but me and your dad are going to visit your grandmother again today."

"Oh, OK," Noah said, a heavy feeling of gloominess settling over him. "Is it her stomach, still?"

"I'm afraid so, love," Mum said. "As soon as we get back, I'll give you a hand, OK? I promise."

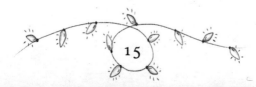

Noah nodded.

"Gemma will help you," Mum said.

Gemma had managed to bring her toe all the way up to her face to get a nice close look.

"Not now, Noah. Can't you see I'm busy?" she said. "Urgh ... I think this is a job for the tweezers ..."

She hopped off the sofa and wobbled upstairs to the bathroom. Noah stared at the box of decorations sadly.

"We should get going," Mum called to Dad. He came out of the kitchen and they both put their big coats on and headed towards the front door.

"There's some bits and pieces in the fridge, pal," said Dad. "Gemma's in charge while we're gone – if she ever comes downstairs, that is."

"We'll get ready for Christmas when we get back home, OK?" Mum added, giving Noah a kiss goodbye. "Be good!"

Noah smiled and waved as his parents left the house. However, as soon as they'd gone, his smile disappeared. It was Christmas Eve, his grandma was ill, the house looked basically the same as it always did, Gemma wasn't interested in helping him decorate and he was pretty much home alone. For

a boy who loved Christmas, things couldn't get much worse.

In the living room, he looked up at the bare tree and then at the empty spot where he usually laid out treats for Santa Claus and his reindeer.

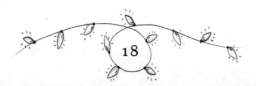

Mrs Jingles rubbed against his ankles, purring for attention. She was wearing a pretty collar decorated with snowflakes, which sparked something inside Noah. If Mrs Jingles could be festive, so could he. He wasn't going to let this Christmas go down without a fight.

"OK, Mrs Jingles, it's just you and me," he said. "I didn't get those decorations down from the attic for nothing. I'm going to make this place so festive, Santa Claus himself would be jealous!"

Mrs Jingles miaowed.

"That's the spirit!" he cried.

First, Noah went to the kitchen to grab some carrots from the refrigerator, to leave out for the reindeer. He also poured a glass of milk for Santa. Next, he dived into the cupboard under the kitchen sink, where his dad hid a secret stash of chocolate biscuits. Normally, Noah and Gemma would bake gingerbread for Santa, but, like everything else, they hadn't done it this year, so Dad's chocolate biscuits would have to do. Then, he took everything over to the fireplace, where he laid it all out in a neat row on the hearth.

"There we go," he said. "That'll keep Santa and the reindeer happy. One Christmas tradition down . . . now for another."

He brushed cobwebs away from the box of decorations and opened the lid. Inside was a sparkly treasure trove of Christmas ornaments, tinsel and fairy lights.

"Ooh," he sighed, pulling out a shiny star-shaped bauble and a round ornament with ballerinas painted on it. "I've missed you guys." He took extra special care with the glass fairy that went on top of the tree every year.

Noah carefully emptied the box until he had all the baubles laid out on the carpet. It would be an epic task decorating the entire Christmas tree on his own – but someone had to do it. He was gathering up the tinsel and the fairy lights, so he could put them on first, when something caught his eye – a decoration in the shape of a gnome. It had a long white beard, a big round nose, a pointy, red-patterned hat with a bell at the tip, a playful smile on its face and an arched eyebrow that made it look like it was about to get up to some mischief.

"I remember you!" Noah said. "You used to belong to Gran when she was little."

He stood up and took the gnome ornament over to the Christmas tree, then reached up to place it on a branch right in the middle.

"It's a shame you can't help me with

the other baubles, Mr Gnome," he said. "I wish everyone was as excited about Christmas as you seem to be."

Noah was just about to drape tinsel over the branches when the gnome bauble suddenly began to glow.

"Huh," Noah said. "That's odd." He turned the bauble around, looking for a switch, but there was nothing at all to show that the gnome was electronic, or that it had any kind of light inside it.

"That's strange . . . you don't have any batteries . . ."

But then something even stranger happened. The light and delicate

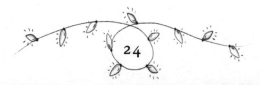

gnome bauble began to grow warm in Noah's hand, and started becoming heavier too.

"This is a definitely a bit odd," said Noah. "What do you think, Mrs Jingles—"

But before Mrs Jingles had a chance to even miaow a reply, a powerful beam of light shot out from the gnome. Noah leapt back in surprise and dropped the decoration on the floor. As he looked down, Noah caught sight of the gnome's cheeky face and gasped. If he wasn't mistaken, the bauble had just *winked*!

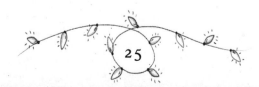

Chapter Two

For a moment, the gnome decoration lay still on the floor, giving off a strange glow. The bell at the end of the gnome's hat began to tinkle and chime, until eventually the ringing became a deafening clamour – so loud that Noah had to cover his ears. Magical light swirled around the gnome, shining brighter and brighter.

What is going on? wondered Noah. If his eyes weren't playing tricks on him, the gnome decoration was **GROWING!** It grew and grew and GREW until the gnome was almost as tall as Noah, its pointy hat just about level with his eyes.

Mrs Jingles had seen enough. She quickly scrambled up the tree and took cover behind the highest branches. Noah's feet were rooted to the spot. He didn't know whether to cry out or just stare in amazement as green, red and gold sparkles exploded out from the gnome like fireworks. And then . . .

DING!

The bells stopped ringing.

The colourful sparkles cleared.

And in front of Noah, the gnome bauble did a roly-poly then leapt proudly on to its feet. Except, it wasn't a bauble any more. The gnome was **REAL.**

"Ahhh – at last!" the gnome cried, stretching his arms above his head, wiggling his fingers and bouncing up and down on the spot. "It's about time someone needed help. Far too much hanging around! My name is Tomte, but you can call me Tommi. What's your name?"

Noah couldn't move his lips. In fact, he couldn't move any of his body. He was stiller than a statue of a very still thing.

"Hmm," Tommi continued cheerfully. "Maybe you didn't understand me. I am from Norway, after all. Are you Spanish? I can speak Spanish too! *Hola!* Or what about German? *Guten tag!* I even have a little bit of Greek . . . Whatever works for you – it's been quite a while since I've spoken to **ANYONE!**"

"No – no," Noah managed, blown away by the gnome's enthusiasm. "English is fine . . ."

"Oh good," Tommi said. "So, your name . . . ?"

"Noah," he said, still in disbelief. "Noah Gibson."

"Noah! I love it! I knew a reindeer once called Noah. Fantastic antlers. However, he was much furrier than you!" Tommi gently pushed back the big red hat that had fallen into his eyes. "Speaking of furry things, who's that hiding in the Christmas tree?"

"Oh, that's Mrs Jingles," Noah said. "My cat."

"I love cats!" Tommi exclaimed, beaming. "I had a pet cat once, but he

ran away and joined
the circus."

Noah wasn't quite sure
what to say to that. He didn't know
that gnomes had pets, or that cats
could join the circus.

"Erm, I'm sure she'll be down
eventually. She's just a bit funny with
new people," he said. "But I don't
understand. Who are you? And what
are you doing here?"

Tommi chuckled, hopping from one
leg to another. He couldn't stand still
for a moment.

"I'm a magic gnome! Have you never

heard of one of those before? It's my job to help make Christmas fun. At least it was – but I got a bit stuck being a bauble. I changed myself into it for a bit of a laugh and, well, I couldn't change myself back until someone said they needed my help."

"I see," said Noah.

"By the sounds of it, you *really* need help," said Tommi. "Which is lucky for you, because I LOVE Christmas – even more than turkeys do!"

Noah wasn't entirely sure that turkeys DID love Christmas, but he decided to go along with the strangeness of it all.

"I love Christmas too," said Noah. "But at the minute, no one else seems that into it. My gran is ill and my sister doesn't want to do anything Christmassy, even though we used to have fun decorating together."

"Well, it's a good job I'm here then," Tommi said. "Together we'll make Christmas more fun than Santa on a sledge in a snowstorm."

Noah laughed. How was any of this possible? Magic gnomes only existed in the Christmas stories his grandma had told him. But this one was right in front of his eyes!

"So where should we begin?" asked Tommi.

"Um . . . the tree, I guess," Noah said. "It **STILL** needs decorating and it's Christmas Eve!"

"Treeeee-mendous!" said the gnome. "That's 'pine' with me. It's good to 'branch' out."

Noah laughed. "So, if you could just grab that box . . ."

Tommi shook his head. "No, no, no. No need for grabbing. I've got gnome magic. Watch this . . ."

Tommi strode forward boldly and looked the tree up and down. Seeing

the gnome coming nearer, Mrs Jingles clambered down the tree, dashed under Noah's legs and hid behind an armchair, her fur bristling.

But the gnome just ignored her. Instead, he gently took his hat off, reached into it and threw a handful of golden dust in the air. The magical dust twinkled all around. Tommi tapped his nose three times and sang a cheerful rhyme:

By the magic of the gnome,

Decorate this Christmas home.

Right before Noah's eyes, the fairy lights floated out of the decoration box

and hung in the air. Tommi raised his arms like a conductor and they flew across the room and began to wrap themselves around the tree.

"Wow," Noah gasped. "That's unbelievable!"

"I think you mean de-**LIGHT**-ful," said Tommi, cracking another cheesy joke. But before the job was done and the lights were turned on,

Tommi's big round nose began to twitch. Something was wrong.

"Uh oh," he said. "That magical dust has gone right up my nose. It's been years since I've used it, you see. Stand back, I think I'm about to . . . to . . .
A-A-A-AAAAACCCHOOOO!"

Tommi let out a gigantic sneeze, which shook the room. The magic sparkles in the air disappeared with a **POOF!** and the fairy lights fell to the floor in one giant tangle.

"Frosty fudgicles!" Tommi cried. He stepped forward to untangle the lights but immediately his foot got caught.

Noah saw exactly what was about to happen.

"Look out!" he cried.

But it was too late. The gnome fell backwards, right on to the decorations Noah had carefully spread out on the living room floor.

CRUNCH! Tommi landed on the glass fairy that was supposed to go on top of the tree, crushing it under his bottom.

"Ouch, that's sharp!" he cried.

"No!" Noah cried. "Tommi, what have you done?"

Tommi looked a little sheepish as he climbed to his feet and brushed himself

down, picking bits of broken bauble out of his bottom.

"Sorry, Noah," he said.

"Mum is going to be so mad!" Noah said, staring at the broken ornament.

"Don't worry," said Tommi. "There's always a way to mend these things. I do have gnome magic, after all."

Noah couldn't help but think that it was Tommi's gnome magic that had got them into this mess in the first place. He picked up the fairy lights and began untangling the knots – at least they hadn't been broken.

While Noah tackled the tangled

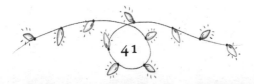

lights, Tommi tried
to fix the fairy. But it
didn't seem to be going
that well. First there was a
flash and the fairy was fixed – but her
wings were stuck to her bum.

"Oops, let me try that again," Tommi
said. But the next time the fairy was
completely blue. The gnome tugged
his beard in frustration. "Now, why
did that happen?" he wondered out
loud. "Hmmm, maybe if I adjust
the spell . . ." He took another pinch of
golden magic dust out of his hat and
threw it at the blue fairy. There was a

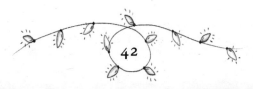

flash of light . . . and she exploded into even more pieces than before!

"Maybe we should put the decorations up *without* magic?" Noah suggested. He began putting the fairy lights on the tree. Tommi came over to help him, and together they hung ornaments and baubles on the branches.

"There," said Tommi, hanging up a snowflake bauble. "That's everything."

Noah counted down from five, just like he would normally do with his family. He felt the usual excitement bubbling up in his belly, then flicked the

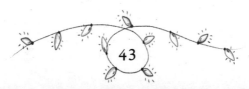

switch. The lights filled the room with multicoloured twinkles.

"Spectacular!" said Tommi. "I couldn't have done it better myself."

Noah nodded. It was beginning to feel a little bit like Christmas. "Too bad we don't have anything to go on top of the tree."

"Leave it to me," said Tommi. "I have an idea!"

Before Noah could even ask, Tommi was dashing across the room. He clambered on to one of the lower branches of the Christmas tree, then began climbing to the top.

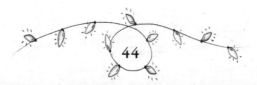

"Tommi, no!" Noah cried. "What in the name of Rudolph the Red-Nosed Reindeer are you doing?"

"Helping, obviously!" the gnome cried as the branches sagged alarmingly.

Noah very much doubted that, but there was no stopping the mischievous gnome. He was almost at the top now, seemingly not bothered at all by the many pine needles that had got lodged in his beard on the way up.

"Every tree needs a fairy," he began. "If I can't fix the one I broke, I will **BECOME** the one I broke!"

"Oh, here we go . . ." Noah said.

Tommi lifted his hat and the room was filled with sparkling magic dust once more. The gnome sat on top of the tree, pressed his nose three times and chanted:

Father Christmas, let me be
The fairy on top of this tree . . .

With a whoosh of magic, Tommi was transformed once more, this time into a fairy that sat at the top of the tree. Only the fairy had a long white beard!

"Ha ha!" Noah laughed. "You look great!"

"Thanks," the gnome said. "I agree. This dress is quite snazzy, isn't it! I can't

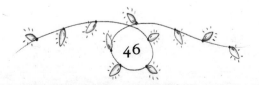

wait to try these wings out."

Tommi flapped his wings energetically and started flying around the living room.

"Woohoo!" he cried, zooming around in circles.

Noah ducked as the gnome/fairy flew over his head.

"Check this out!" cried Tommi. He did a loop the loop, knocking over a lamp.

Noah dived forward to catch it before it fell on the floor. "Careful," he said nervously, setting the lamp back on the table.

"Incoming," shouted Tommi. As he landed back on the top of the tree, it began to sway. Gently at first, then ferociously from side to side. Eventually it swayed too far, and with a worrying whooshing noise, the whole thing toppled over and landed right in the middle of the living room floor with an almighty **CRASH!**

Chapter Three

"Tommi!" Noah cried. "Are you OK?" The gnome magic had stopped working again and Tommi was back to his normal size – and was no longer wearing a dress.

But before Noah could help Tommi up from under the fallen tree, he heard something no little brother wanted to hear when he was surrounded by a

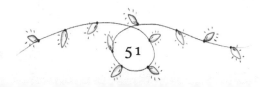

huge mess: the footsteps of his big sister coming downstairs.

"Quick!" Noah said. "I need your help, Tommi!" If Gemma saw the state of the living room, he'd be in BIG trouble.

The gnome climbed out from under the branches and scrambled to his feet. But the footsteps had already reached the bottom of the stairs. It sounded as if Gemma was coming towards the living room. Then the door-handle began to turn—

Noah held his breath. Tommi clutched his beard. Mrs Jingles let out a

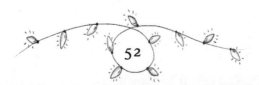

contented purr – she *loved* seeing people get into trouble.

But then the door-handle *stopped* turning. Instead of coming into the living room, Gemma went into the kitchen. Noah heard the fridge door open and close, then the thud of footsteps as his sister made her way back upstairs.

"Phew!" Noah cried. "I thought we were done for."

Mrs Jingles let out a disappointed miaow and went to sulk underneath the sofa.

"Your sister can't really be that bad,

can she?" Tommi asked.

"Well, not normally," said Noah. "Gemma's usually pretty fun to be around – especially at Christmas. But this year she's making the Grinch look friendly!"

"Yikes," said Tommi. "Probably a good thing she didn't come in here then, after all the mess we've made."

We? thought Noah in disbelief.

They each took an end of the tree, and it wasn't long before they'd got it standing up properly again, and at least some of the fairy lights, baubles and candy canes were safely on its

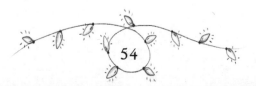

branches. The only thing that was still missing was something to put on top. Noah looked around and found the bauble with dancing ballerinas engraved on it. His grandma had bought it for him the previous year when the whole family had gone to see a production of *The Nutcracker*. Looking at it made him feel sad and worried.

"That's pretty," Tommi said.

"I know," Noah replied, blinking back tears. "The trouble is it reminds me of last Christmas, which was so good. But this one . . ."

Tommi reached up and patted Noah on the shoulder. "This one will be even better, I promise. Watch this."

Tommi raised his hat and tapped his nose three times. Sparkling gold dust flew out from under the hat and landed on the ballerina bauble.

Cheer up, Noah, you will see
How magical Christmas can be . . .

In a flash, one of the ballerinas leapt off the bauble and landed delicately on the floor. She did a graceful pirouette, then danced across the carpet to the

tree. Toes pointed perfectly, she jumped from branch to branch, and when she reached the top, she did a final twirl before freezing in place with her hands over her head.

"Wow!" Noah gasped. Even though Tommi's magic had led to all sorts of chaos before, he couldn't deny how beautiful the decoration was, gazing down from the top of the tree.

"See," Tommi said. "Don't write off this Christmas just yet!"

"I won't," said Noah, beaming. "Your magic worked brilliantly this time!"

"I might look old, Noah," said

Tommi. "But I'm only two hundred and fifty, which is practically a baby for a magic gnome! And I've been stuck as a bauble for quite a lot of those years, so my magic just needs a bit of practice."

Noah reckoned that was fair. It was just like his dad always said – practice makes perfect. And when it worked, gnome magic was pretty cool!

Just then there was a loud rumble. It sounded like the drum section of a marching band, except it was coming from inside the room. Noah looked at the gnome in alarm. Was Tommi doing some more magic?

"Oh, erm, that'll be my stomach," said the gnome. "It's emptier than Santa's workshop on Boxing Day."

"I bet," said Noah. "Do you want a snack? What do magic gnomes like to eat, anyway?"

"Oh, anything," said Tommi. "Potatoes. Boiled parsnip. Bits of old cheese. Crumbs you find down the back of the sofa . . ."

Noah thought for a moment. He didn't have any crumbs on hand, but he might be able to make something better: gingerbread. He and Gemma normally baked some every Christmas.

But this year, what with everything going on, they hadn't gotten around to it yet.

"How about some gingerbread biscuits?" Noah asked. "They're like crumbs, but bigger! And better! I could make some – the only slight problem is I'm not allowed to use the oven without Mum or Dad..."

"Sounds dee-lish!" Tommi cried. "Who needs an oven when there's magic?"

"Well...I suppose..." Noah began.

"Is that a yes, then?" asked Tommi. "Can we make gingerbread men?"

Noah thought for a moment. "Yes – just so long as we don't make a mess—"

But before he could even finish his sentence, Tommi was already bounding towards the kitchen. Noah hoped he hadn't just made a very bad decision . . .

Noah caught up with Tommi just in time to see him climb up on a chair to reach the cupboards. He flung the cupboard doors open and started rooting around to find the right ingredients. He grabbed a bag of flour, some sugar, spices and golden syrup.

"Oopsie!" he cried, spilling some flour on the floor.

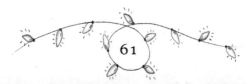

Tommi dragged the chair over to the fridge and took out some butter and eggs. The magical gnome was so excited he began magically juggling the eggs in the air. One of them landed right at Noah's feet with a **SPLAT!**

"Watch it!" Noah cried, leaping back as quickly as he could. "No mess, remember. Besides, these are my special Christmas socks – I don't want to get egg all over them!"

Noah was wearing a pair of thick woolly socks that looked just like reindeer. They even had red pom-poms at the toes to look like Rudolph's nose.

"Sorry, Noah," said Tommi. "I'm just so excited for crumbs. I mean, gingerbread men."

Mrs Jingles came wandering in to see what was going on, just as the magical gnome leapt up on to the counter and began adding the ingredients to a mixing bowl.

"Ah, Mrs Jangles," said Tommi as he stirred the mixture. "Ready to help?"

Mrs Jingles let out a low rumble

from her belly. She obviously didn't appreciate Tommi getting her name wrong. She peered over the side of the mixing bowl, immediately got a puff of flour in her face and began to sneeze.

"Get down from there," said Noah, shooing Mrs Jingles away. He was beginning to feel increasingly worried about the state of the kitchen. "You know you're not allowed to be on there."

Mrs Jingles leapt off the counter and began pacing round the room, leaving a trail of flour paw prints behind her.

"We're nearly done," said Tommi

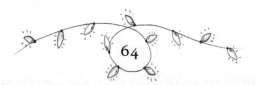

after he'd blended all
the ingredients together.
"Let's roll out the dough!"
Tommi slapped the dough
on to the kitchen counter and
used a rolling pin to bash it into
shape. Noah fetched the cookie cutter
and began cutting out gingerbread
people. Soon, they had a whole batch
laid out on trays.

"All right," Tommi began. "This is the
magic moment . . ."

The gnome lifted his hat and tapped
his nose three times. Golden sparkles
flew out of the hat and landed on the

gingerbread biscuits as he said the
magic words:

Little men all sweet and happy,
Time to bake and make it snappy!

In no time at all, the beautiful scent of
baking biscuits began to fill the air.

"Mmm! It smells like Christmas,"
said Noah. The biscuits started to turn
a lovely golden-brown right in front of
his eyes. "They look ready to me."

"I told you all you needed was a little
bit of magic," Tommi cried, delighted
with himself.

The gnome leaned forward
and picked up one of the biggest

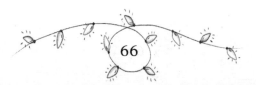

gingerbread men. "I haven't had one of these in years."

But just as the gnome brought the gingerbread man to his mouth, it let out a low growl.

"Put me down this instant, you beardy biscuit muncher!" the gingerbread man shouted.

"**WAH!**" Tommi cried. "What in the name of Santa's knickers . . ."

He dropped the gingerbread man to the floor, scattering crumbs everywhere.

"Be careful, mister," said the gingerbread figure. "You could have

broken me. Do you know how deliciously crunchy and fragile I am?"

Noah leapt back in surprise. Suddenly the mess in the kitchen was the least of his problems. He was more concerned about the fact that a biscuit had just come to life. What next? Were the spoons and bowls about to start talking too?

It wasn't just the one gingerbread man that had come to life, though. The others were getting to their feet as well.

"Ooh, you smell lovely," said one.

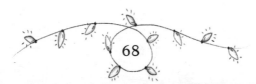

"Nice and spicy. Just the right amount of ginger."

"You too," said another. "You're looking very well baked."

"I'm a bit burnt around the edges," said a third. "But I'll do."

"Pfft – you lot are already starting to go stale . . ." said a fourth.

"Ignore him," said the first. "What a grumbly, crumbly excuse for a gingerbread person."

One by one, each of the gingerbread people leapt off the tray. Noah watched as they climbed stiffly down from the kitchen worktop. They lined up in

formation by the kitchen door, and the first gingerbread man, who appeared to be their leader, began barking instructions.

"OK, gingerbread people, you know the drill . . . If we stick around here much longer, we'll be eaten. That kitty cat has a hungry look in its eyes. I don't trust that gnome as far as I can throw him – everyone knows that gnomes love gingerbread. And who knows what that boy has up his sleeve."

"I don't have anything up my sleeve," Noah said, waving his arm around to show that it was empty. "We're not

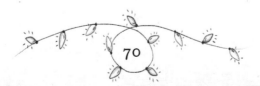

going to eat you, if that's what you're
worried about."

"Speak for yourself," whispered
Tommi.

"Hmmph," said the gingerbread
leader. "That's what they always say.

Gingerbread people, run, run as fast as you can!"

And with that, the horde of gingerbread people dashed out of the door!

Chapter Four

"No, wait, come back!" Noah cried.
But it was too late. The army of
gingerbread people marched out of
the kitchen and straight down the hall.
Noah and Tommi took one look at each
other and ran out of the room as well.
Mrs Jingles followed them – there was
no way she was going to miss out on
the excitement.

The gingerbread army were quick, and in just a few seconds they were rounding the corner and storming into the living room.

"All right, my biscuit-y brothers and sisters," the gingerbread general cried, "spread out. They will never take us alive! We can outwit them if we try – we weren't baked yesterday. Stand firm until the last one of us is dunked into a cup of hot chocolate!"

Noah tried to explain that the gingerbread army had it all wrong. For a start, they hadn't been baked at all – they had been **MAGICKED** by Tommi.

And secondly, they couldn't just go running around his living room – they would get crumbs everywhere. That might appeal to Tommi, but Mum told Noah off about crumbs at the best of times. And what would Gemma say if she came down?

"Tommi, we have to round them up," said Noah. "You grab the biscuit tin – I think there's one back in the kitchen – and I will see if I can catch some of them!"

"I'm on it, Noah," Tommi called.

The gingerbread army quickly fanned out. Some of them dived into

the box of decorations, causing a huge clatter and crash. Others began climbing the Christmas tree as if they were adventurers scaling a dramatic mountain.

"Find higher ground!" shouted the gingerbread general, sending some of the biscuits clambering up the curtain.

Noah spotted one just as it was trying to squeeze into the gap under the sofa.

"Oh no you don't," he said. "If I'm not allowed to leave crumbs everywhere, then neither are you!"

"For the love of shortbread, no!" the biscuit squealed. "Please have mercy!

I'm too young to be eaten!"

"Be quiet, silly!" said Noah. "I'm not going to eat you, all right . . ."

Noah made a lunge for the gingerbread person and grabbed it by the leg before it could get away. Then he shoved the squirming biscuit in to his pocket.

"Now, you just stay there," said Noah. "I've got a whole batch of biscuits to catch!"

Under the tree, two more biscuits were clambering over the presents, trying to find a hiding place among them. They were ruining all the wrapping paper in

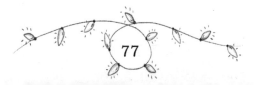

77

the process, ripping it so you could see the presents underneath. When Noah approached, they took one look at him and grabbed a pair of candy canes off the Christmas tree.

"*En garde –* you undercooked digestive!" one cried, challenging him to a duel.

"Show us what you're made of," said the other. "Or are you all flour and no spice, eh?"

Noah picked up a nearby roll of wrapping paper and prepared to do

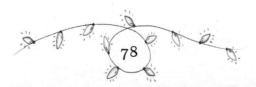

battle with a pair of biscuits – a turn of events he hadn't expected when he'd woken up that morning.

"No one calls me an undercooked digestive!" he cried.

Noah stepped forward and clashed "swords" with the two biscuits. Crumbs went flying everywhere. The gingerbread people worked as a team, one poking at Noah's legs with the candy canes and the other stomping up and down on his toes.

"Ow," Noah cried. "That hurts!"

"Oh yeah, you big Jammy Dodger," said one. "How does it feel being on the

receiving end, eh? How would you like it if **WE** ate **YOU?**"

"But I'm not trying to eat you—" Noah protested. Although he had to admit that they did smell delicious!

It was no use; the gingerbread fighters were quick and nimble and they outnumbered Noah. Once they'd jabbed him a few times with their candy canes, they raced off across the living room. He chased after them but they were just too quick.

"Ha ha ha!" they cried. "Haven't you heard? You can't catch US; we're the gingerbread men!"

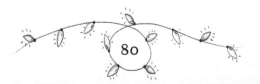

But just then, as they dashed under the coffee table and emerged from the other side, a dark shadow loomed over them – a hungry, furry menace with whiskers, just waiting for its moment to strike. It jumped high in the air and then arced downwards, landing on top of one of the gingerbread people with its teeth clamped around its leg . . .

"Mrs Jingles!" Noah cried.

"It got me!" cried the stricken gingerbread soldier as Mrs Jingles munched on its leg. "This can't be the end – I can't bear the embarrassment of being eaten by a c-c-cat!"

"Get off him, you furry brute!" cried the gingerbread person's fellow fighter, poking Mrs Jingles in the nose with a candy cane. She let out a startled miaow and dropped the biscuit, who hopped away as fast as its remaining leg could carry it.

"Yee-hee!" it squealed. "This biscuit lives to fight another day!"

Noah looked around the living room. He was completely surrounded by biscuits.

"We will never surrender!" cried the gingerbread general. He brandished a candy cane sword. "Troops, get ready to attack!"

Luckily, reinforcements arrived in the nick of time. Tommi came barrelling back into the room brandishing a biscuit tin.

"I've got it, Noah!" he cried. "Now what do we do?"

"Here," Noah said, transferring the biscuit in his pocket into the tin. "We've

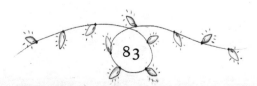

got one; now we have to get the others. But it's proving a little tricky . . ."

"Leave that to me," said Tommi.

The gnome stood in the middle of the living room and began performing his magic once more.

Can't you see the mess we're in,
Get into this biscuit tin!

Golden sparkles flew across the room, out from under Tommi's pointy hat. Suddenly, the gingerbread army stopped what they were doing, transfixed by the magic. Then, one by one, they rose into the air.

"Get that tin ready, Noah," Tommi

said.

Noah knelt on the floor with the tin open and watched in amazement as the gingerbread army floated across the room and landed in the tin in neat rows.

"You'll never get away with this," the gingerbread general said, kicking his legs. "I'm going to report you to the head baker . . . you just see—"

But before he could finish his threat, Noah fixed the lid on tight.

"We did it," Noah cried. "Thanks, Tommi!"

"Team effort," said the cheeky little gnome, giving Noah a high five. "This

should keep them contained until the magic wears off."

Mrs Jingles let out an annoyed rumble from deep within her throat. She had been hoping for a snack.

Now that they'd safely dealt with the gingerbread army, there was just one problem left. Noah looked round the living room in dismay. Some of the presents had their wrapping paper ripped and the floor was littered with broken baubles and crushed candy canes.

"Oh, crumbs . . ." muttered Noah. He meant it quite literally. There were

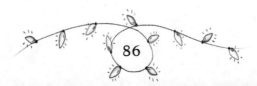

crumbs *everywhere*. "We'll have to clear this mess up before—"

"I can help with that," Tommi said with glee, licking his lips.

Just then the door handle turned, and this time the door swung open. Noah's sister, Gemma, strode through. She looked up from her phone and took one glance around the living room. Then she took off her headphones and fixed her eyes on Noah.

"WHAT HAVE YOU DONE?"

Chapter Five

Noah began fidgeting with his hands as he frantically tried to think of an excuse.

"Erm, it wasn't me," he began, "it was..."

Noah looked around the living room. The gingerbread men were safely locked away in the biscuit tin. Mrs Jingles was lounging beside the fire,

licking crumbs off her paws. Strangely, Tommi was nowhere to be seen.

"It was the cat," he said, laughing nervously. "She had a bad case of the zoomies. She was running around all over the place! I've never seen her move so fast. I think she thought she was in the cat sprint championships or something . . ."

Gemma's eyes narrowed.

" . . . Or, you know, at the cat disco, doing the whiskers waltz . . ."

Gemma's eyes got even narrower.

". . . So, er, yeah, in conclusion, it was the cat."

Mrs Jingles looked up as if to say, "How dare you bring me into this."

"I thought only kittens got the zoomies," Gemma said, suspicious.

"No – no," Noah replied. "Definitely grown-up cats too. It's probably because of her catnip Advent calendar. I let her open one of the doors and it must have made her over-excited."

It wasn't really a lie. Mrs Jingles *did* have a catnip Advent calendar.

Gemma didn't look convinced. "You'd better get this cleaned up. Mum and Dad will be annoyed if the place is a mess when they get back."

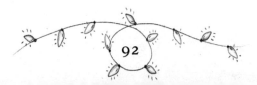

"Don't worry!" Noah said. "It will all be back to normal soon. We promise!"

"We?" Gemma asked.

"Er-er, yeah," Noah stammered. "Me and Mrs Jingles."

Gemma grabbed her phone charger, which she'd come down to get.

"Whatever – just make sure it's done!"

Then she made her way back upstairs, slamming the living room door on the way out.

Noah let out a sigh of relief. Mrs Jingles gave a grumpy miaow.

"Wheeee-oo," Tommi said, crawling out from his hiding place behind the

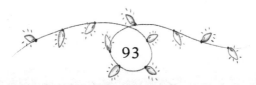

sofa. "*Someone* was in a bad mood! Big sisters are scary!"

Noah frowned. "She's not normally like that. We usually do fun things together at this time of year."

"Well, this year you have me to do fun things with," said Tommi.

"About that," Noah said. "Gemma was right: it is a total mess in here. We're going to have to sort this out before Mum and Dad get back. I'm not sure what to do about all the presents that got ripped . . ."

"Well, why didn't you just say, Noah?" said Tommi. "Let me help . . ."

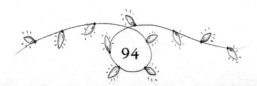

Tommi skipped into the centre of the room, tapped his nose three times and raised his hat with a flourish.

The living room needs a fix,

Christmas magic, do some tricks!

Tommi lifted up the brim of his hat and golden sparkles whizzed out. The living room was transformed instantly. The baubles were back on the tree. Not a crumb or candy cane remained on the carpet. Everything was ready for Christmas.

Noah braced himself for disaster. Were the gingerbread men going to burst out of their tin? Was the

Christmas tree going to topple over again. Something usually went wrong where Tommi's magic was concerned ...

"Why are you looking at me like that?" Tommi asked.

"Because everything looks great," said Noah. "Which is a bit strange, because normally—"

"You're right!" exclaimed Tommi. "I did make a mistake. I forgot to fix the wrapping paper!" He tapped his nose again and released another shower of sparkling magic from his hat.

A roll of wrapping paper printed with Santas and reindeer flew through the

air. In one swift movement, the roll unfurled and sheets of paper tore off it. In a flurry of folding, the gnome's magic quickly re-wrapped the presents under the tree.

"Awesome—" said Noah.

But no sooner was the word out of his mouth than the roll of wrapping paper flew towards HIM! The paper wrapped itself around and around Noah's body, starting with his legs, winding up to his belly and then finally over his head. Soon, the only bits of him that weren't wrapped up were his eyes, nose and mouth. To add insult to injury, the

magic tied a bright red ribbon around his neck and plopped a big bow on top of his head.

Then the same thing happened to Mrs Jingles. All that could be seen was a set of whiskers and a pair of furious yellow eyes. They both looked like fancy Christmas gifts. Or festive-themed ancient Egyptian mummies.

"Tommi!"

Noah cried. "You've turned us into Christmas presents!"

Tommi burst out laughing. "The bow on your head really suits you."

"Don't laugh!" Noah cried. "Get us out!"

"Get yourself out of it," Tommi said. "It's only wrapping paper!"

Noah wriggled and jiggled until the paper started to loosen. Then he punched a hole through the wrapping. Once his arms were free, he tore the paper off his legs. Then he bent down and unwrapped Mrs Jingles. The poor cat looked very confused. Noah picked

her up and gave her a cuddle.

Tommi gathered up the rejected ribbons and, with a flourish of magic, they decorated the walls as festive garlands. "I bet this is the most festive house in the street now," said Tommi, looking pleased with himself.

"I don't know about that," said Noah. "Some people on the street go **ALL OUT**." He went over to the window and opened the curtains.

Tommi clambered up on to the windowsill to take a look outside.

"Ooh," he cooed. "You're right."

Up and down the street there were

lights hanging from the roofs, inflatable Santas waving their arms about in the air and reindeer ornaments perched on front lawns. Compared to them, Noah's house looked a little bare.

"We do have some lights, and there are some decorations in the garden shed," said Noah. "It's just what with Gran being unwell, we haven't had a chance to—"

Tommi hopped down from the windowsill and frowned. "This isn't good. I can't let your neighbours out-Christmas you. What would Santa's elves say if they knew? They

would never let me live it down, not in a million Christmases!"

"It's fine," said Noah, looking around the beautifully decorated living room and, for the first time, feeling a bit of Christmassy excitement. "Everything looks great in here."

"Don't you want to show your neighbours how much you love Christmas?" Tommi asked.

"Yeeesss," Noah replied, already feeling like he was going to regret it.

"And isn't it about time we put a festive smile on your sister's face?"

"Yes!" agreed Noah. He longed for

Gemma to get in the Christmas spirit.

Tommi began racing towards the door, dragging Noah along with him. "Well, in that case, my friend, we're going to make this house less no no no and more **HO HO HO!**"

Chapter Six

Noah grabbed his coat and swapped his slippers for his boots, then rushed out after Tommi, who had already raced down the side alley towards the back garden.

"Wait for me!" he shouted.

Noah followed the trail of sparkly golden bootprints that Tommi had left behind him. When he caught up,

he found the door to the shed wide open and the mischievous gnome rummaging about inside.

"No," Tommi said, flinging aside the lawnmower. "Double no," he huffed, pushing away the deflated paddling pool. "Triple no with mistletoe on top," he cried as he tossed a heavy toolbox out of the way.

Noah winced as it landed with a clatter. The gnome was good at making messes, even when he wasn't doing magic.

"Aha!" Tommi shouted finally as he discovered the box marked "Outdoor decorations" and a huge plastic bag with "Inflatable snowman" written on it. "I've hit the jingling jackpot!"

"Here, let me help you," said Noah. The box was taller than the gnome.

"No need," said Tommi. With one lift of his hat and three taps of his nose, the familiar magical sparkles came rushing out. The magic lifted the box and bag

of decorations out of the shed and
carried them to the front garden.

Noah and Tommi ran around to the
front of the house and delved into the
decorations. There were outdoor fairy
lights, plastic prancing reindeer, icicles
that lit up, a sign that said "**SANTA
STOP HERE!**" and finally, in the
big plastic bag, a gigantic inflatable
snowman.

While Noah set up the plastic
reindeer, Tommi used his magic to hang
the icicles from the roof and drape fairy
lights around a bush. Together, they
set up the snowman in the middle of

the lawn, and Noah inflated it using an air pump. As it filled with air, the snowman's arms waved around. They'd had the snowman for as long as Noah could remember, and it was starting to look rather tired. Noah's arms were starting to *feel* tired too, from all the pumping. "That will do," he said, letting go of the pump. He gazed around, feeling disappointed. The half-inflated snowman looked as though it was melting. Lots of the fairy lights weren't working, their bulbs needing to be replaced. The house was decorated, but it didn't look very impressive.

"Hmmm," said Tommi, peeking over the fence to have a look at what the next-door neighbours had done. The whole front of their house seemed to be ablaze with colour, and their front lawn was like being transported to Santa's workshop.

"That's given me an idea," said Tommi. "I can make this **LOADS** better."

"How?" asked Noah, suddenly worried. Mum and Dad would be back from the hospital soon, and he had to make sure Tommi didn't cause any more mischief. "Maybe things are all

right as they are . . ."

But Tommi took no notice. He stepped forward, tapped his nose and lifted his hat once more. This time he spread his arms wide and cast a magic spell as he spun round and round:

Festive magic twinkle and glow,
Help our Christmas spirit grow . . .

"Whoa!" Noah marvelled as magical golden sparkles swirled through the air like snow and landed on the house and lawn. Suddenly – **PING!** – the whole front of his home twinkled with colourful Christmas lights, and so did every bush, shrub and tree in the front

garden. They flashed on and off like disco lights. Light-up candy canes lined the front path, and nutcracker statues guarded each side of the porch. And if Noah wasn't mistaken, the icicles hanging from the roof were real – and shimmering in the glow of the flashing fairy lights. The front garden looked like a winter wonderland. If that didn't bring a smile to Gemma's face, nothing would.

But the magic wasn't done working yet. The inflatable snowman began to grow too. It was being blown up like a balloon! It grew and grew, until it was

nearly as tall as the house. The reindeer out on the lawn grew until they were the size of **REAL** reindeer. They lost their glossy plastic shine and now had beautiful sleek fur and proud antlers.

"That is so cool!" Noah shouted. "The reindeer are so realistic."

"Not bad, eh," said Tommi, admiring his own work.

A click-clack noise interrupted the two of them, as Mrs Jingles emerged from her cat flap to see what all the fuss was about. She made her way over to one of the reindeer and gave it a sniff. The reindeer scuffed its hoof back and forth on the ground, shook its antlers and let out a deep call as if it was just waking up from a hundred-year sleep.

"Oh my goodness!" gasped Noah. The reindeer didn't just look real. They WERE real. It was like the gingerbread people all over again!

"Be careful, Mrs Jingle Bells," said Tommi. "Reindeer can get a bit grumpy, you know?"

But Mrs Jingles took no notice and paid the price when one of the reindeer accidentally stomped its hoof down on her tail.

YOOWWWLLLL! Mrs Jingles wailed in annoyance. She darted past Noah and took cover under a bush as the reindeer grazed on the grass and nibbled the bushes. One even did a poo.

Mum and Dad are not going to like that, thought Noah. But at least the house looked really Christmassy now.

"I've got to get Gemma down to see this," Noah said. "If this doesn't make her feel festive, nothing will!" Shielding his eyes from the dazzling lights, he glanced up at his sister's bedroom. But instead he saw something very worrying ...

"Um ... Tommi?" said Noah nervously. "Is that snowman ever going to **STOP** growing?"

The snowman had puffed up to the size of a hot air balloon now, towering over the house, and it was showing no signs of slowing down ... It just kept getting bigger and bigger and **BIGGER**.

"Good question," said Tommi. "Let me refer to my magic manual."

"There's a manual?" Noah cried.

"Of course," said Tommi, rooting around in his beard. "At least there was. I must have left it somewhere else. Hmm . . . I'm trying to remember the right spell. I haven't used it in years."

Just then, Mrs Jingles decided to take her revenge on the reindeer who'd trod on her tail. She jumped out and swiped at the reindeer with her claws.

The reindeer reared up in fright and began to chase Mrs Jingles around the garden. The reindeer's hooves churned

up the lawn and knocked down the light-up candy canes.

"Look out," Noah cried, dragging Tommi out of the way just as the reindeer charged past them. "It's out of control!"

Mrs Jingles shot up a tree, but the reindeer was running too fast to stop.

"Oh no," said Noah as he realised what was about to happen.

Its antlers lowered, the reindeer charged right into the belly of the gigantic snowman, and the whole thing exploded with a ginormous **POP!**

Chapter Seven

PFFFFTTTT! With a hiss of air, the inflatable snowman began to shrink. Soon it was just a puddle of plastic on the grass. Mrs Jingles came down from the tree and sat on the deflated snowman.

"So *that*'s how you stop an out-of-control giant inflatable snowman," Tommi cried.

The magical spell was broken. The
reindeer had stopped in their tracks
and transformed back into the plastic
reindeer he had pulled from the shed.
There were still fairy lights decorating
the house and garden, but they were no
longer flashing wildly.

"It's a shame, though," said Noah,
shooing Mrs Jingles away and putting
the deflated snowman in the bin. "It
was pretty cool."

"Hmm, true," said Tommi. "Maybe
we should make a real snowman
instead."

"How can we do that?" asked Noah.

"There isn't any snow."

"That's not a problem for a Christmas gnome!" exclaimed Tommi, raising his hat. "Just you wait and see!"

Soon, he was chanting a spell that sent sparkly gold magic into the sky once more:

North Pole winds start to blow,

Help us now and let it snow!

Noah looked up just in time to see clouds streak across the night sky. The air turned cold, and he had to shove his hands deep in his pockets to keep his fingers warm. Snowflakes began drifting down from the sky. The big

fluffy flakes fell thick and fast, and
in just a few minutes, there was a
blanket of white covering the lawn, the
house and the entire street. The snow
shimmered and sparkled under the
Christmas lights.

"Wow!" said Noah, lying on his back
and making a snow angel. "This is so
cool!"

Tommi beamed with pride.

Just then the front door opened and
Gemma came dashing out. Noah
jumped up and brushed the snow off
him.

"Noah, what was that bang I heard?"

she began. But suddenly she stopped in her tracks. "It's snowing!" She stuck out her hand and caught a snowflake in it. Her face lit up with a big smile. "This is so amazing. It's actually snowing!"

"Cool, huh?" Noah said.

"Yippee!" cried Tommi. "I knew we could make her smile!"

Gemma's smile instantly disappeared. She stared at Tommi, and her mouth widened in shock. "Who. Is. That?" she said.

"Erm . . . this is Tommi," Noah said. "My friend."

"Your friend?" Gemma said, staring

in disbelief. "But he's a . . . he's a . . ."

"A magical Christmas gnome," Tommi said proudly.

"I found him in the decorations box earlier," explained Noah. "I was feeling sad because we hadn't done any of our usual Christmas traditions. I wished that he could help me decorate, and he somehow came to life."

Gemma stepped closer to take a closer look. "I thought I recognised him!" cried Gemma. "He's our old bauble – except much, much bigger!"

Tommi stuck out his hand for Gemma to shake. She took it gently.

"Pleased to meet you, Gemma,"
said Tommi, pumping her hand up
and down enthusiastically. "I'm the
reason why the living room was a bit of
mess earlier. We were battling a whole
gingerbread army."

"A what . . . ?" said Gemma, looking confused.

"You had to be there," said Noah.

"Now, am I right in thinking you are not having the best Christmas this year?" Tommi asked Gemma.

"You could say that," Gemma said, sighing. "I normally love Christmas, but this year . . ."

"What?" asked Noah.

"I'm just worried about Gran," said Gemma. "It feels wrong to get into the festive spirit when she's unwell."

"I know your grandmother very well," said Tommi. "She wouldn't want

you to miss out on having Christmas
fun. It's always been her favourite time
of the year."

"That's true," said Noah, nodding.
"Gran loves Christmas."

"Hang on a minute," said Gemma
suspiciously. "How do you know our
gran?"

Tommi chuckled. "Because when
she was a little girl back in snowy
Norway, we had Christmas adventures
together."

"What?" said Noah. "You didn't
mention that."

"Well, you don't know everything

about me," said Tommi. "I have my secrets. Actually, I'm surprised she hasn't told you about the time I turned her home into a gingerbread house, or the Christmas we visited Santa's workshop together and took his sleigh for a joyride."

"She *has* told us those stories," said Noah. "But I didn't know they were *true*!"

"That's why I'm so glad to be making special Christmas memories for you two as well." Tommi brushed snowflakes off his beard. "Now, why don't we start making that snowman?"

"What do you think, Gemma?" said Noah, turning to his sister. "Do you want to build a snowman with us?"

"Y-y-yes!" said Gemma, her teeth chattering. "But first I need to get my coat – I'm freezing!"

When she returned with coats, hats and mittens for them all, Noah, Gemma and Tommi all got to work. Noah and Gemma each rolled snow into two giant

balls for the body, while Tommi rolled
a small ball for the head. Working
together, Noah and his sister placed one
big ball on top of the other and put the
little ball on top.

"I know what we need," said Noah.
He dashed back inside to grab a carrot
to use for its nose.

"Good thing there aren't reindeer
running around any more," said
Tommi. "Or they'd eat that straight
away."

"Reindeer?" said Gemma, looking
confused.

"Don't worry," said Noah, glancing

over at the decorations on the lawn. "It's all under control."

"What can we use for eyes?" asked Tommi.

Noah found spare buttons in his coat pocket to use for eyes. Then he found some small pebbles and used them to make a mouth. Tommi found two twigs to use as arms.

Gemma fetched an old pair of headphones from her bedroom. "Now he can listen to some cool Christmas tunes."

"Awesome," said Noah.

Tommi walked around the snowman, adjusting bits here and there, trying to make it perfect.

"It's good," he said. "But I think it could be better . . ."

"Uh oh," said Noah. "I know what that means . . ."

Tommi raised his hat and tapped his nose three times, and magical sparkles came flying out from under it . . .

Help us make this snowman be
The most magical we'll ever see!

The sparkles swirled around the snowman. Christmas carols started

playing loudly from the headphones.

"What's happening?" said Gemma.

"It's gnome magic," said Noah. "Let me guess – it's going to come alive." *And probably make a mess*, he thought.

Right in front of their eyes, the snowman began to transform. The twig arms waved hello. The button eyes blinked at them. The pebble mouth curved into a smile.

"Oh, wow!" gasped Gemma.

"See," said Tommi. "I told you it could be better."

The magical snowman peered at the two children and the little gnome.

Then, with a jolly laugh, he bent and scooped snow up off the ground.

"Er, what's he doing?" Noah asked.

The snowman rolled the snow into a ball. Then he rolled another, and another.

"He must be making a little snowman," said Gemma.

But that wasn't it. With a merry grin, the snowman launched the snowball straight at them. It landed with a cold **SMACK** right in Noah's face.

"He's starting a snowball fight!" Gemma cried.

"Let's get him!" shouted Noah.

Chapter Eight

Laughter filled the air as Noah, Gemma and Tommi dashed around the front lawn, forming snowballs and throwing them as quickly as they could. But no matter how fast they worked, the snowman was faster.

Pow! Pow! Pow! The snowman hurled snowball after snowball at them. Noah ducked, feeling one graze the very top

of his head as it whizzed through the air.

Gemma let out a squeal as another splattered against her legs. And Tommi got hit by one right on the nose.

"Hey," he shouted, wiping snow off his face. "Now my nose is cold!" The

gnome turned and tried to run away
– and another chilly snowball hit him
right on the bum.

"Ouch!" gasped Tommi, clutching his
bottom.

"You did ask for it," Gemma said,
giggling. "It was your magic after all."

Noah, Gemma and Tommi pelted the snowman with snowballs, but the snowman fired huge boulders of snow back at them.

"We need to work together," shouted Noah. "It's the only way we can win."

"Take that!" Gemma cried, hurling a big, fat snowball right into the snowman's mouth.

Noah picked up three snowballs and hurled them in quick succession. They splatted on to the snowman with a satisfying **THWACK**.

Even Mrs Jingles got in on the act. She leapt up and pawed at the snowman, as

if he was a frosty scratching post.

"He's weakening," shouted Noah as the snowman started to slow down. "Let's finish him off!"

Tommi leapt forward, tipped his hat and tapped his nose. Then he quickly came up with a spell.

We've had enough, it's time to go,
Magic, melt away this snow!

In an instant the snow that had blanketed the garden disappeared. The snowman began to melt, the three balls getting smaller and smaller and smaller, until all that was left of him was a carrot, two twigs, two

buttons, a pile of pebbles and some old headphones.

"That was amazing!" said Gemma, panting.

Noah grinned. He had loved every second of the snowball fight with his sister. It had been just like old times. He picked up the carrot that used to be the snowman's nose. "I'll put this with the reindeer treats by the fireplace," he said.

"Speaking of treats . . ." Gemma said. "Who wants hot chocolate?"

"Me!" cried Tommi.

"Me too!" said Noah.

Even Mrs Jingles let out a miaow that seemed to suggest she was up for hot chocolate. All four of them hurried inside together to get warm.

But as soon as they were back in the house, hanging up their coats, Noah noticed the headlights from their parents' car as it swung into the driveway.

"Oh no!" Noah gasped. "It's Mum and Dad! They're back." He stared at Tommi, wondering how on earth he could explain the gnome's presence.

"Quick," Gemma said, ushering him into the living room. "Hide behind

the sofa. Until I figure out what to tell them."

The little gnome shook his head. "I'm not going to hide," he said.

"But Tommi," Noah said, "What will Mum and Dad say?" While his parents hadn't said *not* to bring any Christmas decorations to life, he was pretty sure it was against the rules. He and Gemma weren't even allowed to invite friends over when their parents were out.

Tommi smiled at them. "I'm not going to hide because it's time for me to go. I came here to make sure you both got into the festive spirit, and now my work

146

is done. Besides, I need to recharge my magic."

Noah's smile disappeared. He'd hoped Tommi could stay around a little bit longer.

"But I promise I'll be back," said Tommi. "Whenever you need a little bit of gnome magic. OK? Remember – all you have to do is ask for help."

Noah nodded.

As the keys turned in the door, Tommi tipped his hat once more, tapped his nose and released a flurry of sparkling Christmas magic that filled the whole house. Before their eyes, he turned back

into a Christmas ornament.

Noah picked him up off the floor and held him in his hand. He missed his gnome friend already.

Mum came bursting through the door and straight into the living room. "Hello, you two," she said. "I love what you did outside. The lights look—"

But before she could finish her sentence, she stopped and looked around the living room in amazement. When she'd left, the tree had still been bare. Now it was covered in baubles, tinsel, candy canes and fairy lights. Garlands hung from the walls, brightly

wrapped presents sat under the tree ready for Christmas morning and Santa's snacks were laid out ready for his visit.

"Oh my goodness," Mum said. "Did you two do all this too?"

Noah wasn't quite sure what to say.

"Well, kind of," he said. "But there was definitely a little bit of Christmas magic involved as well."

Mum beamed. "It does look magical in here. What a wonderful surprise to come back to. Thank you both."

"But Mum," said Gemma. "What about Gran? Is she OK?"

Mum took a deep breath. "Well, now it's my turn to surprise you two . . ."

Just then, Dad came through the door, ushering someone in with him.

"GRAN!" Noah and Gemma shouted, rushing towards her. "You're here!"

Noah and Gemma's grandma opened her arms wide and gave them both a great big hug.

"My two favourite little mince pies," she said. "What have you been up to? This place looks amazing!"

"What have *you* been up to, Gran?" said Noah. "We thought you were ill."

At that, Dad rolled his eyes and dramatically cleared his throat.

"Go on," he said. "Tell them."

Gran gave Dad her own little annoyed glance.

"Well, you know how I had all that trouble with the pickled herring that time? Ever since then my stomach's been a little off. But I *so* wanted to start

on the Brussels sprouts. I know it was a few days early, but I couldn't help myself . . ."

"And how many did you eat?" asked Dad, even though he knew the answer very well.

"Oh, shush, you," she said. "It wasn't that many. About fifteen. Maybe twenty. Twenty-five at a push . . ."

"Twenty-five!" Noah roared.

He and Gemma collapsed into giggles.

"But they were so delicious, and after all, it is nearly Christmas," Gran said, trying to defend herself.

"Yes, well, they'll be having a very stinky Christmas in hospital this year after your visit!" Mum teased. "Anyway, I'm glad you're back home, on Christmas Eve, where you belong. Now, who wants gingerbread? Shall I make some?"

"Oh, erm, Gemma and I made some when you were gone," Noah said.

"Did we?" Gemma said.

"Yes!" Noah said, nudging his sister in the side. "Remember, we made a whole **ARMY** of them. You said they tasted **MAGICAL**."

"Oh yes, of course!" Gemma said,

playing along. "How could I forget?"

"That explains the lovely smell in here," said Mum. "I can't wait to try them." Shooing Mrs Jingles out of the way, she reached down to the coffee table where Noah had left the biscuit tin.

Noah held his breath as she opened it, half expecting the gingerbread general to launch another attack. That would be all they needed – a whole gingerbread army escaping and running riot around the living room.

But when Mum looked inside, there were just neat rows of biscuits.

"They look delicious," she said.

Noah breathed a sigh of relief.

"Who wants hot chocolate?" said Mum. "Your dad and I will get that ready. You two keep Gran company."

Mum and Dad hurried off to the kitchen, and Noah and Gemma helped get Gran settled in the chair by the fire. Mrs Jingles took up her familiar place on the rug. She looked tired out from all the magical adventures and was soon purring in her sleep.

As they all settled down, Gran noticed something that Noah was still carrying around in his hand.

"Ah!" she gasped. "My Christmas gnome . . . I haven't seen him since I was a little girl."

"You remember him?" asked Noah.

"Remember him? Of course! Tomte and I had so many adventures together." She gasped and clapped her hands. "I'll bet you had an adventure with him, too, didn't you . . ."

Noah and Gemma shared a smile and let their grandma in on the secret.

"And did he cause any mischief?" she asked.

"Lots!" said Noah.

"Ah well, he's definitely the same old

gnome I remember from when I was a girl, then."

At this, the bauble version of Tommi gave a little wink.

"What should I do with him?" asked Noah.

"Well, put him on the Christmas tree, of course!" said Gran, laughing.

Noah made his way across the cosy living room to where the tree stood proudly. The smell of hot chocolate was beginning to waft through from the kitchen. But Noah was already feeling warm inside, from being surrounded by the people he loved most at the most

magical time of year.

Standing on his tiptoes, Noah put Tommi up on one of the highest branches, facing back out into the room so their gnome friend could see all the Christmas fun.

"Happy Christmas, Tommi," whispered Noah. "Something tells me this is going to be the best one ever!

THE END